The Buddha's Diamonds

CAROLYN MARSDEN
AND
THẦY PHÁP NIỆM

CANDLEWICK PRESS

First paperback edition 2010

The Library of Congress has cataloged the hardcover edition as follows:

Marsden, Carolyn.
The Buddha's diamonds / Carolyn Marsden and Thầy Pháp Niệm.
—1st ed.
p. cm.
Summary: As a storm sweeps in, Tinh's father tells him to tie up their fishing boat, but the storm scares him and he runs away. When the damage to the boat is discovered, Tinh realizes what he must do.
ISBN 978-0-7636-3380-6 (hardcover)
[1. Fishers—Fiction. 2. Responsibility—Fiction.
3. Family life—Vietnam—Fiction. 4. Vietnam—Fiction.]
I. Niệm, Thầy Pháp. II. Title.
PZ7.M35135Bu 2008
[Fic]—dc22 2007023025

ISBN 978-0-7636-4828-2 (paperback)

10 11 12 13 14 15 BVG 10 9 8 7 6 5 4 3 2 1

Printed in Berryville, VA, U.S.A.

This book was typeset in Sabon.

Candlewick Press
99 Dover Street
Somerville, Massachusetts 02144

visit us at www.candlewick.com

For the community of Deer Park Monastery

C. M.

For my cousin Thy Mai

T. P. N.

CHAPTER ONE

In the gloom of the dusty temple, Tinh bowed to the Buddha. Three times he knelt, touching his forehead to the grass mat. Then he stood with his palms joined in front of his heart, regarding the statue: reddish copper beneath the layer of grime.

The Buddha's right hand rested in his lap, close to the earth, while the other was raised in the mudra for peace. The Buddha, with his full cheeks and almond eyes, looked something like Ba, Tinh's father.

Tinh's cousins—Trang Ton, Dong, and Anh—also bowed, not so quickly that the adults would make them prostrate again, but with no time wasted. They longed to get outside before the monk began his long talk.

Several side altars were laden with vases of sweet jasmine and offerings of globular green guavas and waxy star fruit.

One altar, half-hidden by the donation box, displayed photographs of the village ancestors, including Tinh's grandparents—Ong Noi and Banoi. Tinh's gaze lingered on the small faces in the black-and-white photos. Both grandparents had died not long ago, and Tinh missed them.

Tinh looked out at the temple courtyard shining with morning sunlight. His cousins would soon head for the open field beyond.

Trang Ton had just gotten a new soccer ball from his rich uncle in America.

Yet when Tinh's cousins finished bowing, he didn't follow them, but settled himself onto the floor beside Ba and Ma.

The monks and nuns, with their shaved heads and loose brown robes, waited cross-legged at the front of the temple. A very old monk sat in the middle.

From outside, Tinh heard the shouts of the little kids fighting their mock battles, using long stems cut from elephant-ear plants and soft old coconut husks that they tossed from behind the temple walls.

Lifting a wooden baton, a nun invited the temple bell, a large ceramic bowl. The bell vibrated in low, penetrating tones.

Each week Tinh waited for this moment when the world and his heart settled.

Even the little soldiers outside silenced their shouts. After the nun invited the bell twice more, women raised their palm-leaf fans, waving them gently.

The monks and nuns started their chant: "*In the precious presence of the Buddha, fragrant with sandalwood incense, we recognize our errors and begin anew. . . .*"

The words entered Tinh like soft rain.

"*The raft of the Buddha carries us over the ocean of sorrows. . . .*"

Tinh sighed, the knots inside him relaxing.

When the chanting stilled, the old monk began his talk: "Today I offer you a handful of diamonds. Not one diamond, but a handful."

Expecting to see real jewels, Tinh looked up. But the monk opened his hand to reveal nothing.

"You may think we have little in our village," the monk continued. "You may think that we should be sad to be so poor. But we have the sun." He pointed overhead. "And the moon, the source of all poetry." He pointed upward again.

As the monk talked, Tinh studied pictures depicting the life of the Buddha. The scenes were painted on the eastern wall: the Buddha as a baby taking his seven famous steps, a lotus blooming in each footprint. The Buddha as a young prince. The Buddha reaching enlightenment under the bodhi tree with its green-heart leaves.

"You have the diamond of your mother. Even if your mother has passed away, you have her within you. You have the diamond of your father. . . ."

The monk's voice was like the ocean at low tide. Tinh shut his eyes and let the words paint pictures in his head.

"The sea full of fish, the fresh winds, the breath flowing in and out of your body—all these things are beautiful diamonds in your life, shining day and night. The Buddha offers you these diamonds of true happiness. . . ."

"Go look after your sister," Ma whispered. She leaned over Tinh, her long bangs grazing his forehead.

"Now?"

"I'm afraid she'll be bullied. Or she might get hurt," Ma insisted.

Tinh got up and stepped out of the temple, blinking in the bright light.

"Where have you been?" asked his little sister, Lan. Her legs were thin below her too-short dress.

"I stayed for the talk."

Lan wrinkled her nose. "Make me a kite,"

she said. She held out two pieces of bamboo and some pink paper, a bit of string, and a bottle of glue.

"You brought everything," he said.

"I remembered what you needed."

Tinh stood on tiptoe and looked toward the soccer field. If there was a soccer game going, he certainly didn't want to spend time with his sister. But it was probably too late to join the game. Plus his cousins would tease him for staying in the temple.

Tinh sat down on a low wall and fastened Lan's bamboo sticks into the shape of a cross. When the sticks were firmly tied, he held the skeleton of the kite to the sky, imagining it floating in the soft blue.

Lan wiggled in anticipation.

As Tinh lowered the bamboo to his lap and

stretched the pink paper over the cross, he thought of how the next day his sister would run along the beach, flying this kite.

Last summer, Tinh had also flown kites. But when he'd turned ten at Lunar New Year, he'd left that childhood behind. Now, during the long days of summer vacation, it was his job to help Ba with the fishing.

"Hold here," he said to Lan.

Lan put her small finger on the paper while Tinh glued.

"You need more string for a tail," he said when the paper was in place. "And some bits of cloth to tie on to the string."

Just then, Tinh heard the shouts of Trang Ton, Dong, and Anh and then someone shushing them. Then, Tinh heard another sound—like a giant mosquito. He stood up to look.

Zooming ahead of the four boys came a

miniature red car. Tinh stepped back. The car drove itself. It ran up the dusty path and across the flagstones of the courtyard as if by magic.

The little kids stopped their war games to watch.

Adults leaned out the temple doors, fingers to their lips.

"Want to try, Tinh?" Trang Ton held out a small gray box. "Here, you just push this button to go forward, this one to go back. These"—he touched two more buttons—"make the car go left and right."

Tinh reached for the remote control. It was heavier than it looked. He tapped the button on the left, and the car drove toward a palm tree. He maneuvered the car around the base of the tree. He drove it to the edge of the stone steps, then backed it up. He loved the feeling of power in his hands.

“Now it’s my turn,” said Phu, one of Trang Ton’s younger cousins.

Tinh handed over the box. This car was a diamond the monk didn’t know about.

No one in the village could afford a remote-controlled car. Trang Ton had an uncle who’d escaped by boat to America. That uncle worked in an office and sent back money and gifts like the soccer ball and the car. The uncle’s generosity enabled Trang Ton’s family to live in a brick house instead of a hut made of bamboo.

The bell sounded three times, and Phu held his finger over the remote control, poised for action. All eyes were on the red car, now half-submerged in a pile of faded bougainvillea flowers.

The vibrations stopped, and Phu backed the car up.

The adults emerged from the temple, talking and laughing among themselves.

As the nuns spread a feast of fruit on a long table set up in the courtyard, Tinh turned his attention from Trang Ton's red car. He loaded his arms with vanilla mangoes, finger bananas, a stick of sugarcane, and a bunch of longan.

He plucked a round longan fruit from the stem and sunk his teeth into the hard skin. The fruit burst open, white and sweet.

CHAPTER TWO

The next morning, Tinh's golden boat left the shore, the engine running hard. He watched the village of Hai Nhuan grow smaller and heard the shouts of the little boys playing soccer on the beach grow fainter.

He saw Lan running with the dogs and other children, flying the kite, a pink triangle against the dark *cay duong* trees. The trees dropped long needles onto the sand.

Now, seeing the flashes of bright paper in the sky, he almost longed for his old life of playing all day.

Though the sky still glowed with early light, the air felt unusually hot and still. The diesel fumes from the boat's engine lingered, mixing with the smell of salt.

Circling lazily overhead, some seagulls, *chim hai au,* waited for fish to be caught in the nets.

Tinh turned his gaze to the far horizon and the adventures that lay beyond. Every now and then a big wave would surge out of the ocean. Tinh always scrambled to the bow, the most exciting spot, as the boat rode over the wave.

The golden boat was new. The old one had rotted with the seawater and tropical heat. This one was five times as long as Ba, seven times as long as Tinh. It was so new that the bamboo shone golden against the turquoise water.

Second Uncle had helped Ba build the boat. When it was finished, Tinh had rubbed sticky water-buffalo manure over the cracks, sealing them. The manure smelled very strong. When he was almost finished and Lan had called him to hunt shells, he'd gone with her.

When Ba found out that Tinh had left some of the gaps unsealed, he'd shouted, "You're foolish to be afraid of a bad smell, Tinh. Our boat could sink because of your carelessness!"

So Tinh had rubbed on more manure until no more light showed through the bamboo.

Then he'd glued two conch shells on either side of the prow. The shells symbolized the eyes of a dragon, guiding the boat, protecting it from being tipped over by huge fish.

On the first trips out, Tinh had been seasick, vomiting over the side. But now his body had grown used to the movement of the ocean.

He was glad he wasn't seasick anymore. After his mistake with the manure, he wanted to do everything right on the boat. He wanted Ba to be proud of him. Maybe one day Ba would make this boat his.

Just then, Tinh's cone-shaped hat blew off and landed in the water.

With his fishing pole, Ba lifted the hat out of the sea and handed it to Tinh. "You're day-dreaming again," Ba said. "When the boat is moving, pay attention."

"Yes, Ba." Tinh put on his hat, now dripping, and sat up straighter.

Soon, the boat had traveled so far out that Tinh couldn't see the bamboo huts of the village or even the shore. Only water lay around them, shimmering under the sun and the crystal-blue sky.

Ba shut off the engine. All grew quiet.

A statue of a woman named the Bodhisattva of Compassion, *Phat Ba Quan Ahm,* was tied to the bow of the boat. The Bodhisattva had one thousand arms reaching out to all those in need. Tinh hadn't counted the arms of the statue, but it had many, some hidden behind the others. On the palm of each of those thousand hands, *Phat Ba Quan Ahm* had an eye to watch over those who suffered.

While the Buddha felt like a father, the Bodhisattva of Compassion was a mother, nurturing and protecting everyone, including Tinh and Ba and the rest of the fishermen.

Tinh lit a stick of incense and placed it in front of her smiling face. He pressed his palms together and bowed.

Tinh helped Ba tie two nets to the boat. The small one, like a hammock, caught *ca nuc,* tiny silver fish. The large one drifted farther and captured not only *ca nuc* but also *ca kinh,* diamond-shaped fish, and *ca ngu,* gray fish as big as Tinh's leg.

They also used fishing lines. Tinh cast his line over the side of the boat and waited. As soon as he and Ba caught a few fish, they'd cook soup and eat it with rice wrapped in fresh banana leaves.

This evening, Ma and Lan would be waiting on the shore for the return of the boat and its pot of soup.

Tomorrow, Ma and Lan would load the catch of fish into the *ganh hang,* a contraption of two baskets tied to each end of a bamboo pole. They'd carry the fish to the village of Phong Chuong to sell. With the money, Ma would get rice, vegetables, and rubber sandals. Just before Lunar New Year, she'd buy cloth to make new clothes.

Tinh wished he could buy a remote-controlled car like Trang Ton's. Maybe someday he and Ba would catch so much fish there'd be money not only for necessities, but for such a toy as well.

If the nets could just haul in a little more, Tinh thought.

Ba caught a fish and reeled it in. Moments later, Tinh caught a *ca kinh*. It flashed and twisted, dangling from the end of the line.

By lunchtime, they had enough fish for the soup. Ba poured diesel over the wood in the round metal stove and lit a fire.

While Ba cleaned the fish, Tinh put the pot of water on to boil and added fishsauce, salt, hot pepper, and mushroom powder.

Ba slipped the fish into the pot.

Tinh cast his line again. A wedge of black clouds had formed on the horizon, far out to sea. A shadow passed over his heart. "Look, Ba. A storm."

Ba looked and frowned. "We'll fill the nets before we turn back," he said firmly. "Those are only clouds, Tinh. Rest now and relax."

Tinh nodded, daydreaming of the way the red car had responded to his every command. He pulled his cone-shaped straw hat over his face and lay back. He listened to the gentle lap of the water, his line drifting.

The sky was unusually quiet, though. Now no seagulls flew overhead. Tinh slid his hat back and took a peek.

The blue sky had grown murky yellow as though coated with a film of diesel smoke. Tinh sat up. The wedge of clouds had advanced, becoming darker, bigger.

He peered overboard, searching for the nets. Would Ba decide to go home soon? If there were big waves, Tinh might be sick again. Besides, Ma and Lan would worry. Many afternoons Tinh had stood on the shore while storms were brewing, anxiously watching for the return of Ba and his boat.

Tinh checked the soup, lifting a bit of fish onto the spoon.

Gusts of wind swept across the water, rocking the boat back and forth. Water sloshed in.

Tinh held the pot steady on the stove. Lan would be disappointed if the soup tipped over.

Shielding his eyes, Tinh scanned the ocean. What were the other fishermen doing? Were his uncles and cousins heading for shore?

He spotted Trang Ton's green boat. Trang Ton's nets rose and fell over the waves.

Tinh studied the boats carrying the divers who searched for shellfish on the ocean bottom.

The body of each diver was covered with tattoos to scare away the big fish. The divers stood together, as if talking. One pointed to the sky.

"Let's reel in the lines," Ba said. But he didn't turn the boat around.

Tinh eyed the storm clouds curling like black dragon breath over the ocean.

The boat rose over a huge swell. But this time, Tinh didn't run to the bow for the ride. His stomach churned with seasickness. He thought of a long-ago storm that people still talked about in which many boats, many men and boys, had been completely lost.

Tinh sat low and chanted the name of the Bodhisattva: *"Phat Ba Quan Ahm, Phat Ba . . ."* He prayed that she would reach out one of her thousand arms to protect the bamboo boat.

Ba gripped the edge of the boat and stared at

the clouds. He wet his finger and held it up, testing the direction of the wind. "Let's bring in the nets," he finally said.

Together, they pulled the nets from the sea into the boat. The nets were half empty and light. Out of the water, the fish flopped, their eyes wide.

Tinh felt like a fish himself, tossed and confused. For a moment, he was sorry for the fish and considered throwing them back.

Starting the engine, Ba said, "Steer us toward shore, Tinh."

Tinh held the tiller, but with the waves slapping the sides of the boat, his thin arms couldn't hold the course. Ba had to sit on the other side and help.

The water was dense green. By now the clouds had climbed over the sky. They blocked the sun. Tinh saw all the fishing boats turning back.

In the afternoon darkness, oil lamps were being lit along the shore.

Suddenly, the ocean heaved up, knocking over the pot of soup, dousing the fire. Oh, thought Tinh, his mother and sister would go hungry!

Another wave loomed—a small shark silhouetted in the glassy curve—and slammed Tinh against the side of the boat.

Ba reached out to yank him upright.

The wind screamed as it carried sheets of water back and forth across the ocean.

As the boat was swept closer to shore, Tinh saw the beach crowded with families—including Tinh's many aunts, uncles, and cousins—scanning the wild sea for returning boats.

Lan's pink kite was caught in a *cay duong* tree.

A thick green wave reared up behind them.

Steering the boat was nothing like driving a remote-controlled car!

"Ba!" Tinh cried.

Like a rampaging dragon, the water hurled the bamboo boat onto the sand.

A second wave knocked the boat sideways, and Tinh fell onto the beach.

CHAPTER THREE

"Get up," Ma said, shaking Tinh's arm.

He spit sand from his mouth, blinked sand from his eyes. He heard shouting. He wanted to get up, but felt heavy, as though completely filled with sand.

"More big waves are coming," Ma insisted.

"Hurry," said Lan, leaning over him, her thin eyebrows pinched together.

Tinh sat up. He saw whirlwinds of paper and leaves crossing the beach. The tall coconut palms swayed. The ocean was full of pieces of wood, old coconut husks, and other trash.

More boats arrived. Some dragged their nets behind them. People yelled to one another. Trang Ton and his older brother, Linh, yanked on the nets, trying to keep them from tangling.

"Please stand," said Lan, pulling on Tinh's hand. "Please!" Her voice rose.

A wave swept up. Tinh grabbed for Lan. The water carried her out. She screamed. Her little head bobbed as the wave swelled.

"Ba! Ma!" Tinh called, charging into the green water.

Another wave brought Lan back, depositing her on the sand. She cried and held her leg, which was now bleeding. "Something cut me," she wailed.

The deep gash was jagged. Behind her, Tinh saw a board, adrift in the foamy surf, a bit of rusty metal attached.

He hadn't listened to Lan and now she was hurt.

Ba gathered Lan into his arms and staggered to the dry sand. "Were you daydreaming again? Why weren't you watching out for her?" he called to Tinh.

"I . . ." Tinh began. But he had nothing to say.

Ma followed Ba, her head lowered against the wind.

Tinh followed, too—poor Lan!—but Ba shouted back over his shoulder, "Take the boat higher, Tinh. Get Trang Ton and your uncles to help you."

Tinh watched his family disappear through the *cay duong* trees and into the jungle beyond.

Lan's accident had been his fault. How badly was she cut? He was left behind, all alone. He felt like sinking down, letting the wind ride over him. But now Ba had made him responsible for the boat.

He spotted it among the others, pitched about by the muscular waves. He scanned the beach. Who could he ask? It took four people to walk the boat up the sand. Who could help him?

Third Uncle's boat had flipped over in the water. Tinh's uncles and older cousins were swimming out to bring it in. And two other cousins were still at sea, their boat a black dot chugging toward shore.

Trang Ton, his shirt unbuttoned and flapping, came running toward Tinh.

Tinh cupped his hands to his mouth and called out, "Can you help me with my boat?"

Trang Ton took a few steps in Tinh's direction, but then his mother beckoned him.

"We need you here, Trang Ton," she called.

Trang Ton lifted his hands as if to apologize, then turned away from Tinh.

Everyone was busy.

The ocean looked like a pot of soup ready to boil over, sloshing this way and that, a turgid dark green.

Tinh made his way to the boat and held on tight to keep it from being washed out to sea, to keep himself from running away.

He hadn't taken good care of Lan. But he should at least rescue the statue of the Bodhisattva. He should untie her and take her to dry land.

He heard screams. People pointed. Tinh turned to see a giant wave—almost as tall as the palm trees—arching above the horizon, reaching toward the beach. He abandoned his boat and *Phat Ba Quan Ahm*. He ran along with everyone else. When the wave was about to strike, he held tight to the trunk of a palm tree.

The wave shattered, shaking the earth, creating a world of white foam. It climbed high onto the dry sand, reaching forward. When it retreated with a loud sucking sound, Tinh looked around for his boat.

So many boats had been flung onto the beach, so many floundered in the water, that at first he couldn't see the golden bamboo. But there it was—a few steps away, lifted up the beach to the line of *cay duong* trees. Tinh smiled with relief. The boat was safe now, wasn't it?

Others were not so lucky. Even Tinh's aunties

had to wade into the raging waves to rescue boats. He needed to help them. He walked toward the water.

Another wave gathered itself as it rolled toward the shore. It reared up, bottle green and treacherous, as high as the first. More people screamed and fled.

Tinh hurried along the sand, past the line of *cay duong* trees. Then he looked back—was his boat still on high ground? But instead of the boat, he saw—nested in the sand, completely helpless—Trang Ton's red car. He ran back and grabbed it before the wave broke.

As the earth quaked, Tinh clutched the car tightly to his chest. He clutched it harder as the wave slipped up behind him, reaching for him hungrily. Then he dashed away from the beach and the angry ocean.

He dashed past the canal where people tied boats. Past the bamboo houses and the school and the tiny stall that sold brown-sugar candy.

Everywhere, families called to loved ones, urging children inside.

Finally, Tinh reached his own house, long and low under a thatched roof, a guava tree growing in the front yard. He looked through the doorway of the kitchen building, which was outside the house, and saw Ma standing over a cooking fire. The wind carried the smell of rice soup cooking, this time without fish.

There was no sign of Lan.

Tinh looked down at the car in his hands. Ba mustn't see it. He'd wonder why Tinh had rescued a toy at a time like this. Tinh tucked the red car behind a bush.

"Help me with the sandbags, Tinh," Ba shouted over the roar.

Tinh held the burlap bags open, and Ba shoveled in sand. The wind howled around them, carrying sand from the shovel.

"How is Lan?" Tinh yelled into Ba's ear, the approaching storm roaring.

"Cut."

"Doctor?" Tinh screamed.

"Not now," Ba screamed back.

Tinh opened a new bag. First he'd abandoned Lan to the waves, then he'd left the boat. Ba hadn't asked about the boat. He'd blamed Tinh for Lan's cut. What would he think of the way Tinh had left the precious boat?

He'd abandoned the fishing boat, had taken a toy home instead.

He should tell Ba. But as he tried to speak, the wind stole his words.

When the bags were full, Ba tied a long rope onto each.

Only Tinh was light enough to go on the roof without damaging the thatch. He climbed up a branch of the guava tree, then onto the layer of palm fronds.

Ba threw him the end of a rope.

The wind tore at the thatch, and fronds had already blown loose. As Tinh worked, he hung on tight so the wind wouldn't knock him to the ground below.

He knelt, wishing that he could see the beach and the boat from here. Had the wave carried it high enough? Had the second huge swell taken it out to sea? How many more giant waves had pounded the beach?

He wished he had a thousand eyes to see all that was happening.

He wished he could close his eyes and see nothing.

Once the rope was over the roof, Ba ran to the other side of the house and tied the loose end to another sandbag. The crisscrossing ropes, weighted by the sand, would hold the thatch in place.

They worked on in the wind: two ropes, three . . .

Then the wind paused and the rain began, the first fat drops splatting on the palm fronds.

CHAPTER FOUR

Ma had bandaged Lan's leg with one of Tinh's shirts. Blood seeped through the cloth, and Lan limped to her spot on the sleeping mat.

Tinh bit his lip. "I'm sorry, Lan," he said. "I should have gotten up from the sand faster."

Lan, as though to forgive him, laid a hand on his shoulder.

Tinh lay down beside her. But he couldn't sleep with the wind rocking the bamboo house.

Lan clung to him.

Suddenly, the sky erupted, casting down a sheet of rain. The world outside became nothing but the crash of water. The air in the room grew sticky.

"I'm scared," whispered Lan. "Let's go to Ma and Ba's room."

Tinh helped her up. They walked through the middle room, past the family altar, to stand in the doorway of their parents' room.

"It's only a storm, Tinh," Ba grumbled. "The war was much worse."

But this wasn't a normal storm, Tinh thought as Lan cuddled up to Ma. He'd never seen such a storm. He sat down and pulled his knees up, making himself small.

"Don't turn off the lamp tonight," Lan begged.

So the flame of the oil lamp burned on within its cone of glass.

The thunder knocked the sky open. The thunder reminded Tinh of the bombs that fell in the war. The war had stopped soon after Lan's birth, but Tinh would never forget its sounds. He covered his ears and shut his eyes hard.

The rain drove like long needles trying to penetrate the palm-frond roof.

Lan leaned up on her elbow. "Couldn't we go to Trang Ton's house?"

Tinh listened for Ba's answer. Trang Ton's brick house with the clay-tile roof was strong enough to protect them. Maybe he and Trang Ton could even wait out the storm by playing with Trang Ton's marble collection.

"It's too dangerous to go now," Ba answered. "*Phat Ba Quan Ahm* will take care of us here."

As though proving Ba wrong, the wind suddenly tugged at the palm fronds on the roof.

Tinh stared up, hoping the ropes would hold. But no. The fronds ripped loose. Tinh heard the swish as they sailed into the night.

When rain streamed into the bedroom, Lan began to cry.

Ba picked her up and stood just holding her, as though uncertain.

Surely now, Tinh thought, Ba would take them to Trang Ton's house.

But Ma said, "Come, Tinh. Let's go to the room of the ancestors," and Ba carried Lan to the middle room.

It was very black.

Ba set down Lan and returned with the oil lamp, still burning in its glass, a small world apart from the wild night.

No one slept. Lan tossed, her face damp with sweat. Ma and Ba sat with their shoulders touching.

Tinh paced back and forth, every now and then pausing in front of the ancestral altar.

There were photographs of the ancestors along with offerings of miniature bananas, sticks of incense, and bright red flowers that Tinh had gathered that morning. The petals drooped. Would the ancestors have protected the house better if he'd searched harder for fresher blooms?

The pictures of Banoi and Ong Noi were placed in front of the other photographs. If his grandparents were here now, Tinh thought, wouldn't they be able to help?

On a smaller, lower table in front of the altar stood a statue of *Phat Ba Quan Ahm*. Sometimes Ma let Tinh dust her. He was always careful when wiping the pale green stone, the delicate face with its half smile.

When Tinh thought of how he'd deserted

the Bodhisattva along with the boat, he looked away.

During Lunar New Year, Tinh and his grandmother used to prepare a special tray of food. First, they'd gathered leaves of all shapes and colors of green, blooms of fluted hibiscus and golden jasmine, arranging them in a circular pattern on the round tray. Then Banoi helped Tinh place cups of pudding, bananas, and morsels of brown-sugar candy among the flowers.

Finally, Tinh had held still while Banoi lifted the tray onto his head.

He'd stood for a quarter of an hour under the blue sky, balancing the offering to the Bodhisattva of Compassion.

Banoi had sat nearby, smiling.

Tinh had felt *Phat Ba Quan Ahm* come to him. He'd felt her in the sunshine and in the breeze that tickled his cheeks. She manifested in the ripple of sun and shade under the trees. He sensed her in the air he breathed as he presented his sweet gift while the round shadow of the tray fell over his shoulders.

He saw *Phat Ba Quan Ahm* in his grandmother's shining eyes.

Tinh's grandfather used to take Tinh and his boy cousins to sleep on the beach at night. They'd lain, looking into the sky while Ong Noi talked about the stars and how they moved in relation to the rise and fall of the ocean.

Sometimes they'd gazed out to sea. As the night fishermen cast their nets and lines, the excited fish bumped against each other, creating a green glow in the black water.

Ong Noi also told war stories. Once when the soldiers burned a hut, the tree next to it had burst into white blossoms from the heat. Ong

Noi opened his hands slowly, showing how the flowers had bloomed as the hut fell into a chaos of red embers.

"May the Buddha bless us with peace from now on," he'd said at the end of each story.

When Ong Noi's stories were finished, they'd slept, cradled by the sand. Now, Tinh thought of how the beach, once a refuge, was being pummeled by a furious sea.

Ma lit stick after stick of incense, placing them in a bowl of sand. As she prayed, her lips moved silently.

Breathing in the thick, sweet smoke, Tinh thought again of the boat. Had the ocean pushed it higher, thrusting it among the *cay duong* trees? Had *Phat Ba Quan Ahm* taken care of it? Or had the waves devoured it?

Ba had expected him to be a man, but Tinh had acted like a boy.

Without the boat and daily catch of fish, the family would have nothing. Tinh looked at his sister's small face, white in the glare of the lightning.

No vegetables. No rice. No clothes. And definitely no remote-controlled car.

They'd have *almost* nothing. Pink sweet potatoes grew in the village of Hai Nhuan. At least they'd have those, Tinh reminded himself.

Thunder exploded overhead, shaking the house. Lan cried out.

Tinh thought of Trang Ton's red car hidden in the bush. At least he'd saved that. But a small bit of plastic wouldn't feed a family.

When Ba found out, he would speak harshly. He might lift his hand to hit Tinh. He would make Tinh feel small.

The night was dangerous. But Tinh had to

know where the boat was. Maybe he could even save the statue.

Before anyone could stop him, Tinh darted across the room into the black night.

Ma's voice followed him like a chant: "Tinh! Tinh!"

He heard someone—probably Ba—chasing after him. Tinh ran faster. He ran past the bush where the car was stashed.

Ba mustn't catch him. Tinh had to learn the worst before his father did.

Tinh ran first one way and then another, lost in the angle of the rain. The wind sounded like a horde of demons. Tinh's head spun when the lightning flashed, as it shouted, *This way! No, that!*

All around, tree trunks snapped. Big trees that had once marked pathways crashed to the ground. Raindrops pelted Tinh like small pebbles.

Finally, he heard sharp knocks and the sound of splintering. He'd reached the canal where boats were tied. The hulls banged against each other, cracking apart.

The beach was to his right. In the whirl of the darkness, the ocean threw its weight, over and over, onto the sand. The earth trembled as each wave hit.

The boat? How could Tinh find such a small thing now? How could he find anything as tiny as a statue? His task was impossible. And yet he had to search. He crawled on hands and knees through the wind and rain.

A coconut landed in front of him. Another hit the back of his leg, and he gasped.

It was no use: the wind and rain conspired with the night to hide the boat.

For the second time, Tinh turned away from the beach, away from his boat, his heart churning like the waves.

At least he had the red car. He could hide it behind the altar where Ba never looked.

In the darkness, he ran through the branches of a fallen tree, fighting his way in the snarl of leaves. Twigs tore at him, scratching his skin.

Then he tripped and fell hard onto his chest. The breath knocked out of him, Tinh lay without moving, his tears mixing with the muddy water. The rain drummed on his back.

When lightning struck the ground ahead of him, Tinh saw Ba coming toward him. He jerked himself to his feet.

"Come home now!" Ba shouted.

Tinh stood still, waiting for Ba to grab him.

As they approached the house, Ba's fingers

biting into his arm, Tinh saw the faint glow of the oil lamp through the window.

He saw the silhouette of Ma waiting outside. "Tinh!" she cried. "Oh, Tinh, you are safe!" She held out her arms.

But Ba pushed Tinh past her, and they entered the house, panting, puddles forming where they stood while Lan stirred in her sleep.

Ba folded his arms across his chest. "Where did you go?" he demanded. "Your mother called you back. You disobeyed her."

Tinh put his hands on his knees, bending over, breathing and dripping. This was the right moment to tell Ba everything. But Tinh felt seasick, as though he were on the boat, rocking uncontrollably, tossed by the night.

"Shhh," Ma said to Ba, pushing her wet hair off her forehead. "Our son is home now.

Here, Tinh." Ma sat down and patted the spot beside her.

Ma, like the Bodhisattva of Compassion, beckoned him. But how could Tinh go to her with Ba watching? More than anything, Tinh wanted to crawl across the mat, muddy and wet, to snuggle close to Ma.

But Ba expected him to be a man, helping to take care of Ma and Lan in the storm. Tinh couldn't seek comfort like a child anymore.

He went to the opposite side of the room, far away from Ma, *Phat Ba Quan Ahm*, and the altar of the ancestors, to sleep alone.

CHAPTER FIVE

Tinh woke to the roosters' crowing. Sunlight fell through cracks in the roof, streaking across the ancestral altar. He covered his eyes against the light, then sat up, remembering the storm.

His chest was bruised from the fall, his arms and legs scratched and dirty.

No one else was in the room.

What had happened while he slept? He wandered to the doorway and found Ma sitting on the step, looking out at the yard.

The sun shone over a world in shambles. It took Tinh a moment to make sense of the confusion before him. "Oh, the guava tree!" he suddenly cried. The tree had fallen and the green fruit lay scattered. The leaves were already wilting.

Ma nodded. "The poor dear. She gave us so much fruit."

Looking beyond, Tinh saw other trees down, including the one with the long yellow leaves. He glimpsed the wreckage of houses, now just bamboo and thatch in the tangled jungle. Tinh felt tangled, too. Overnight, all had changed.

"Only the palms and bamboo are still standing," he said.

"That's because they bend with the wind," Ma replied.

Tinh shielded his eyes and peered in the

direction of the bush that sheltered the toy car. He glimpsed a bit of red. But the car wasn't his. He'd have to return it to Trang Ton.

"Where's Ba?" Tinh asked. Had Ba gone to look for the boat? Had he discovered Tinh's carelessness?

"He took Lan to a doctor in the next village. She was feverish. Her leg is infected." Ma pressed her face into her hands.

Tinh sank down beside her. Just yesterday, Lan had run on the beach, flying the pink kite. If he'd only gotten up when she'd asked him to, she wouldn't have pleaded with him. She wouldn't have been in harm's way. If Lan's leg didn't heal, how could she help Ma carry the fish to market?

If there were fish to sell. He had to know about the boat.

Ma looked up again and, putting her hand

on Tinh's knee, said, "This reminds me of the war. After the soldiers came through, ransacking our village, or after a bombing, we had to rebuild our lives. We had almost nothing, but each time we recovered."

Tinh sighed. Ma didn't know about the boat. Recovering without it would be hard. "I'm going down to the beach," he said, standing up. "I'll check on the boat."

He walked out of the yard slowly, hands in his pockets. As though nothing was wrong. He didn't want to worry Ma. But once out of Ma's sight, he ran.

He sank ankle-deep in the puddles. At first, he stopped to shake the mud from his sandals, but soon gave up and went on, muddy to the knees.

He passed houses lying in ruins, leaped over trees fallen across the road. A pig wandered through the remains of the candy stall. Chickens—their feathers bedraggled—roosted in fallen trees. Everything smelled wet.

Second Aunt and her three children stared at the sky. First Aunt and her husband tugged at the rubble. Tinh heard crying and the sharp bark of angry words. Everywhere, he heard the whoosh of brooms sweeping water.

Swarms of mosquitoes attacked Tinh's ankles.

From far off, he could see the ocean, still restless, yet sparkling again, an innocent blue.

At the beach, the *cay duong* trees lay full-length across the sand. Tinh recognized the pink paper of Lan's kite still caught in the long needles of one tree, now fallen.

Broken boats lay underneath the trees. Broken boats were scattered over the beach. Flies gathered on the dead fish still caught in the nets. Tinh held his nose.

He spotted a cluster of boats, jumbled on top of each other. There—could it be? On the bottom? He ran and knelt to touch the golden bamboo, now coated with a layer of white sand. A crack ran through the hull, a wound like that on Lan's leg. The engine was buried in sand.

The Bodhisattva was trapped underneath.

Tinh started to dig with his hands, but with the boats on top, it was no use.

He tried to lift the uppermost boat off, but it was too heavy.

He slumped, his face in his hands.

Just yesterday, his golden boat had glided over the turquoise ocean. Just yesterday, he and Ba had caught fish and all had been well.

Now everything was lost.

With a round thud, a coconut fell to the ground.

CHAPTER SIX

"Tinh!" a voice called.

Tinh looked up to see Trang Ton spinning his soccer ball on one finger.

The ball gleamed black and white in the sunshine, untouched by the storm.

"How about a game, Tinh?"

Tinh gestured toward the rubble covering the beach. "How can I just *play*?"

"Why not?" Trang Ton twirled the ball.

"I need to get my boat out."

Trang Ton stepped closer to the pile. "Isn't that yours on the bottom?"

Tinh nodded.

"There are,"—Trang Ton counted—"seven boats on top. You can't do anything now. You have to wait for the other people to come first." He paused. "Let's go."

"It's easy for you to play," Tinh said. He noticed that Trang Ton was wearing a new striped shirt. "You have a rich uncle."

Trang Ton spun the ball again. "That's true, Tinh. But you'll still be happier if you come with me."

Tinh looked around at the soft blue sea and clear sky.

Suddenly, he thought of the monk's talk. It was true that the sun was still in the sky. He even saw a pale moon. He was still breathing. As were Ma and Ba and Lan.

Maybe Trang Ton and the monk were right. In spite of the storm, Tinh could be happy. He still had a handful of diamonds.

His heart, knotted in fear, unfolded.

But how could he leave this spot? Leaving, he'd abandon the boat for a third time.

"Let's go," Trang Ton repeated. "No one is going to do anything with these boats today, Tinh. They have to fix the houses first."

Tinh indeed saw no one. He got up and followed Trang Ton, his heart like a boat buried in sand.

Dong and Anh joined them. They threw the ball back and forth as they walked, dancing to avoid the puddles, daring each other to jump high over fallen trees.

But Tinh marched with his hands behind his back. What would Ba do when he saw the boat?

A green snake slipped through the mud, and Tinh jumped back.

As the boys approached the temple, Tinh saw that the soccer field was clear. No trees had blown across it. The hot sun had almost dried it. The place lay ready, like an invitation.

But Tinh wasn't ready. How could he play soccer? What would Ba think to see him kicking the American ball while their boat lay at the bottom of the pile?

Tinh noticed that a tree had crashed over the temple, smashing the clay-tile roof.

Had the inside of the temple been damaged by the storm?

Tinh thought of the monks and nuns chanting "*From the mud of adversity grows the lotus of joy. . . .*" Could the Buddha lighten Tinh's heavy heart?

"Where are you going, Tinh?" Trang Ton called. "We're starting the game."

"Play without me," Tinh called back.

He mounted the temple steps, climbing between the stone dragons still standing on guard, their stone fire unquenched.

No one was in the temple.

Rain and wind had scoured the paint from the plaster of the eastern wall, so that Tinh saw only fragments of the Buddha's life.

He stepped onto a floor covered with crushed fruit and flowers, small branches, leaves, and mud mixed with the ashes of burned incense. As he leaned down to pick up the pictures of Banoi and Ong Noi, an incense holder rolled toward him.

Tinh placed the photographs of his grandparents back on the altar and set a wilting blue passionflower in front of them.

The donation box lay on its side in a corner, coins spilling onto the floor.

The once-dim temple was now flooded with light streaming through the broken roof.

Tinh's gaze lifted to the statue of the Buddha towering over him.

The Buddha sat solidly, his eyes half-closed, undisturbed by the night's storm. In fact, he'd been washed clean by the rain and was now lit by fresh sunshine.

Although Tinh's boat had been buried and the village lay in ruins, the Buddha smiled serenely.

Although Tinh's guava tree was down, the Buddha didn't care that his own offerings lay scattered.

All had gone wrong, but the Buddha was still happy.

For a moment, Tinh perceived that happiness

as a soft golden aura, the light of the sun itself expanding from the Buddha's body.

He even felt the beginnings of a glow around his own heart.

But, thought Tinh, that was only his imagination. The Buddha was only a statue created by a sculptor many years ago. His chiseled smile meant nothing.

He listened to his cousins kick the American ball, calling to each other. They and the Buddha were wrong to be happy today. Wrong. Tinh refused to look at the Buddha's face. He turned away from happiness and started home.

CHAPTER SEVEN

At the house, Tinh heard crying from the kitchen. He followed the sound to find Ma sitting by the earthen rice jar.

She held up a handful. "The lid blew off. Our rice is ruined! How will I feed you children?" She faced him, her cheeks wet with tears.

Tinh wanted to hold his nose against the smell of the wet rice that had rotted so quickly in the heat.

"At least we have the guavas, Ma," said Tinh, kneeling beside her. His belly rumbled with hunger.

"Our dear tree," Ma cried harder.

"And we always have sweet potatoes." Tinh laid a hand on Ma's arm.

Ma wiped her cheeks with the back of her hand.

Had *Phat Ba Quan Ahm* forsaken them? Had her thousand arms been busy elsewhere?

Ba would expect Tinh to be the man until he returned. "I'll find food for us," Tinh said to Ma. "I'll take care of us." If he found food, it would help make up for his cowardice with the boat.

He took a bowl from the shelf in the kitchen. "Don't worry," he said, leaving the yard.

With the sun higher in the sky, the air had grown steamy. Tinh wiped his forehead with the hem of his shirt.

He went to Third Aunt's house. The leaves of the banana trees had been torn into ribbons. All was silent. Was no one home?

"Third Aunt, it's me, Tinh," he called out. "Do you have any dry rice?"

Third Aunt came to the door, her hair loose from its tight bun. "I'm sorry, Tinh. Our rice was knocked over by the wind. I borrowed from your father's uncle."

She stared at his empty bowl. "I'm sorry," she repeated.

Tinh set off for First Uncle's house, tapping the bowl against the side of his leg. He passed the school. Chickens pecked in the puddles, and two white dogs scrounged for food.

In the tall palms, birds sang as though the storm had never happened.

As Tinh rounded the bend in the path, he came to First Uncle's house. One wall had fallen in. Leaning on his cane with one hand, First Uncle pulled at pieces of bamboo and palm fronds with his free hand. He moved unsteadily, having lost a leg when he'd stepped on a land mine after the war.

Tinh walked into the yard, carrying his bowl in front of him.

First Uncle glanced at the bowl and shook his head. "I just gave my last rice away, Tinh."

"I hope you saved some for yourself."

"No, children need food more than I do." First Uncle stroked his long, narrow beard. "Ask your aunt who lives in the brick house."

He meant Trang Ton's mother.

As Tinh walked on, he wondered if Trang Ton and the others were still playing soccer.

Fourth Aunt's beautiful brick house was splashed with mud. Clay roof tiles lay on the ground. Sticks floated in the brown sea flooding the yard.

Trang Ton's older brother, Linh, appeared in the doorway.

Recalling the small green snake of the morning, Tinh stopped before the mud. "Do you have dry rice?" he asked, gesturing with the bowl.

"We can give you a little." Linh eyed the huge puddle. "Come around to the window."

Tinh stepped lightly over the wet ground. His family would eat after all.

He held the bowl to the open window while Linh scooped in rice. At the sound of the dry grains, Tinh's stomach clenched. When a few grains dropped into the mud below, he almost sank to his knees to gather them.

On the way home, Tinh stopped off at First

Uncle's house. "I have rice now, Uncle. Let me give you some."

First Uncle held out a coconut shell while Tinh poured in a few spoonfuls.

"Keep this for yourself," Tinh cautioned. "Don't give it away."

"Thank you, Tinh," said First Uncle. "This reminds me of how we used to share during the war." He reached into his pocket and brought out a pendant of green stone, a tiny Buddha. "Here, take this." He laid the pendant on top of the rice. "The Buddha will bless you, Tinh."

"Thank you very much, Uncle."

Tinh carried his bowl of rice with both hands, balancing his family's food and the image. He looked ahead and stepped carefully around debris fallen across the road.

Once he stopped to gaze at the Buddha, sea green against the white grains. The Buddha was seated on a lotus throne, the soft petals supporting him. Tinh thought of how the lotus grew only in thick, dank mud.

In the distance, Tinh saw Lan and Ba walking toward him. He squinted—Lan had a new bandage on her leg.

"The doctor gave me a shot!" she called out when they drew closer.

"Did it hurt?"

"A little. But now I feel better."

A wisp of breeze touched Tinh's cheek. "I'm so glad, Lan," he said.

"I see you found rice," Ba commented. "And the Buddha besides."

Tinh lifted the bowl proudly and smiled. But then he remembered. He lowered the rice and looked at the ground. "Our boat . . ." The rice in his hands suddenly seemed insignificant.

"I've seen it," Ba said. He sighed, and Tinh

felt as though the storm was hitting all over again. "Go on ahead, Lan," said Ba. Then, as Lan limped off, he said to Tinh, "Why didn't you tie it?"

Tinh clutched the bowl. He had to tell Ba the truth. "I didn't ask anyone to help me bring the boat onto the beach," he began. "I . . ." He swallowed hard. "I ran away. A big wave came and I got scared." He didn't mention the red car. He kept his eyes on a line of ants crossing a log. He wished he were an ant.

"That boat is our only way of making a living. . . ."

Tinh drew a circle in the damp ground with his toe. "I know."

"Then why didn't you make sure it was safe?"

"The waves were so big, Ba. . . ." His father hadn't seen those waves.

Ba just squinted, as though trying to see something in the distance.

"Everyone's boat was damaged," Tinh continued. "None was safe."

Ba grunted and said nothing.

Tinh felt smaller than an ant.

That evening as the smell of cooking rice filled the yard, Tinh took the red car from the bush. It was splattered with mud but otherwise seemed unhurt.

Tinh rolled each wheel against his palm. He needed to give the car to Trang Ton, but not yet.

He hid it back in the bush.

The next day, Tinh and Ba mended the roof. First they untied the sandbags and loosened the ropes over the thatch. "Without these ropes," Ba said, "we might have lost our whole house."

Tinh smiled a little. Was Ba saying he'd done a good job with the ropes? Did he feel bad about his harshness the day before?

As though to make up for its own destructiveness, the wind had blown down some palm fronds they could use to repair the roof. Tinh dragged them like huge feathers across the yard.

This time there was no guava tree for Tinh to climb. Ba stood on a coconut tree stump and helped Tinh reach the roof.

From high up, Tinh had a view of the jungle and the ruined bamboo houses tangling together.

He leaned down while Ba handed up the palm fronds.

Tinh lashed the fronds, one by one, with rope made from palm leaves. He tied each knot tight against the next storm.

* * *

A day later, a crowd gathered at the beach to repair the boats. People carried a collection of hand tools: drills, screwdrivers, saws. Trang Ton's grandparents came to watch, sitting in the shade of the coconut palms.

Trang Ton and Linh tossed the soccer ball back and forth. Trang Ton hit it once with his head.

The waves caressed the beach as though to soothe it. When Tinh looked out at the glinting turquoise ocean, it seemed to wink at him with a thousand eyes. He could hardly imagine it rearing up against them all, a ferocious green dragon.

When Trang Ton tucked the soccer ball under a bush, Tinh thought of the red car. "I rescued your remote-controlled car from the beach," he said.

Trang Ton shrugged. "It won't work anymore. The batteries in the remote got wet."

"You can't dry them out?" Tinh asked.

Trang Ton shrugged. "The inside of the remote is green and corroded. You can have the car if you want."

"I can *have* it?" Tinh asked. Was the diamond falling into his hands so easily?

Trang Ton nodded.

Tinh gave a low whistle. But then he quickly realized that without the remote, the car wouldn't run. It would be just a child's toy. He might as well give it to Trang Ton's little cousin Phu.

Tinh helped Trang Ton, Linh, Fourth Uncle, and Ba lift off the top boat. Though the paint was peeling and the shrine had fallen off, the body seemed undamaged.

Tinh watched as the boat was carried to the

ocean. Fourth Uncle tugged at the line of the engine. The engine sputtered once, then roared, letting out a cloud of black smoke. Everyone cheered.

If only it were so simple with *his* boat, Tinh thought. He scratched away at the nest of sand it lay in.

Fourth Uncle and Linh took off aboard the first boat. "We'll catch fish for all of you," Linh shouted over the sound of the engine.

Another cheer went up from the beach. Tinh's mouth suddenly watered. The supplies of rice in the village were almost gone.

The next boat needed more work. The engine had broken off. Dong used the hand drill while Trang Ton dug out the accumulation of sand in the bottom of the boat.

Tinh searched for lost bolts in the sand.

"We're missing all but two," Dong said, and

Tinh searched deeper until he found five bolts, the threads gritty with sand.

He wouldn't rest until his own boat was floating on the ocean again. It would be a while before he'd be able to work on it. To distract himself, he pulled the remnants of Lan's pink kite from the fallen tree. One piece of the bamboo frame was broken. He tore the paper loose from the other piece and laid it aside. When Lan's leg healed, they'd build another kite.

Soon the second boat was also launched. It, too, would bring fish for the village.

Up and down the beach as far as Tinh could see, more boats were taking to the water.

Finally Tinh's bamboo boat lay alone, half buried in sand. Everyone else was either already at sea or repairing other boats, so Tinh and Ba worked alone.

In any case, Tinh thought, with some people

already fishing, everyone's stomachs would be full tonight.

At first, Tinh used a stick, while Ba used the shovel. But when the boat was almost freed, they dug with their hands so they wouldn't damage the bamboo. Sand lodged deep under Tinh's fingernails.

They yanked the boat from its bed of sand and stood back to survey the damage: the once-golden bamboo was gray. The hull was fractured. The engine was packed with sand.

Ba kicked at a rock and said a bad word.

Tinh clenched his fists so the fingernails bit into the palms. How could he and Ba repair all this?

They flipped the boat over. Fish, rotting in the nets, stared at Tinh. They'd died for nothing. If he'd set them free when the storm hit, the Buddha might have blessed him with better fortune.

Then he saw the statue of the Bodhisattva still lashed to her shrine. Tinh untied her and, cradling her in his arms, ran to the ocean. He bathed the statue and dried her with his shirt. He set *Phat Ba Quan Ahm* in the shade, smoothing the sand around her.

Tinh made a sling of his shirt and carried water to wash the boat.

Ba looked over at Trang Ton's green boat, and Tinh followed his gaze. Trang Ton and an uncle were pushing it into the waves.

"Go fish with Trang Ton if you like," said Ba. "He could use your help."

It would be fun to go with Trang Ton. They could have a fish-catching contest. They could tell ghost stories.

But Tinh needed to work on the boat with Ba. He needed to be a man. "I'll stay with you," he said to Ba, meeting his eyes.

Ba gave a tiny nod. A pulse of cool air from the ocean caressed Tinh's cheek.

After Ba cut away the damaged bamboo, Tinh helped to fit in new pieces. Tinh drilled holes with the hand drill. Ba pounded short lengths of bamboo into the holes. Tinh sawed the bamboo nails even with the surface.

Ba drained the diesel from the engine into coconut shells. He handed Tinh a screwdriver to take apart the engine. Tinh laid each piece carefully on a length of cloth. Together, they cleaned off the sand, using rags soaked in diesel.

When all the parts shone, Tinh's breathing softened.

"The boat will never be as beautiful again, but at least it'll be whole," Ba said as Tinh glued on the conch-shell eyes.

"Yes," said Tinh, daring to smile at Ba. "Our boat is a diamond."

Ba grunted, but also smiled.

"Where's the propeller?" Ba suddenly asked.

The propeller was no longer attached to the engine. Tinh glanced around the beach. He saw a bit of metal poking through the sand where the boat had lain. "Maybe here," he said to Ba, and began digging.

The propeller revealed itself little by little.

Ba dug, too, but it was Tinh who cut himself on the jagged edge. When he lifted the propeller free, blood ran down his wrist.

Ba grabbed Tinh's hand. "Careful this doesn't get infected like Lan's leg."

But to Tinh, only the boat mattered now.

The propeller looked like a huge metal flower, one petal twisted, another gashed.

Ba turned the propeller around and around. "We can't fix this."

Tinh's lower lip trembled. The repairs had gone well. And now a problem . . .

"In Phong Chuong there's a machine shop," Ba said. "The propeller will cost precious money to repair, but there's no other way. I can't go tomorrow because I need to take Lan to Dien Hai to be checked again by the doctor."

Phong Chuong lay on the other side of the sand dunes. Tinh had never gone so far all by himself. A trip to Phong Chuong would have been fun with Ba at his side. But alone?

Tinh sucked his cut finger. He'd been careless enough to injure himself. How could he travel so far as Phong Chuong without Ba?

And yet if he got the propeller repaired tomorrow, he and Ba could be out fishing one day sooner. They'd be able to feed Ma and Lan. Ba would be proud of him.

Tinh took the propeller from Ba. "I'll go to Phong Chuong. I'll take the propeller to the men to fix."

"Alone?" Ba asked. "That's a long walk for a boy your age."

Tinh sat up taller. "I'm growing up now. If I'm old enough to fish on the boat, I'm old enough to get it repaired."

That evening, Tinh handed the red car to Phu. "It doesn't drive by itself anymore," he said, "but if you want it, it's yours."

Phu's eyes grew wide. He took the toy with both hands and cradled it close.

"I'm too old for it now," Tinh explained. "I have a fishing boat to take care of."

CHAPTER EIGHT

The next morning, Tinh set off for the village of Phong Chuong. He wore his cone-shaped straw hat and carried a bag containing two pink sweet potatoes wrapped in banana leaves, water in an old soda bottle, and the propeller. Deep in one pocket was the money Ba had given him. Deep in the other was First Uncle's green Buddha.

As he left Hai Nhuan, Tinh passed the cemetery in back of the village. Banoi and Ong Noi were buried here. He'd been sad when they'd died. But by now they'd turned into trees or stars, or maybe ocean waves. Knowing that, Tinh felt better.

Wilted flowers lay strewn around the gravestones. Everyone was too busy attending to the living to tend the dead.

Coming home tonight, he'd have to go by this cemetery again. Ghosts would be out. Unhappy, hungry ghosts who hadn't been cared for. Tinh shivered at the thought. Silently, he chanted: *"Phat Ba Quan Ahm, watch over me. Phat Ba Quan Ahm . . ."*

He entered the region of the sand dunes. The light brown sand was flecked with gold shining in the sunlight.

Before Tinh was big enough to go to market with Ma, he'd waited here in the sand dunes for her return in the evening. When he saw her, he'd run to check the buckets of her *ganh hang* for a special treat: a lump of brown-sugar candy, a mango or banana, or maybe an ear of roasted corn.

Now as Tinh walked to the top of a dune, his feet crunched in the dry sand. In the damp of the dune valleys, mosquitoes bit his ankles.

With every step, he felt the slap of the pendant in one pocket and the rustle of money in the other. What if someone tried to take the money from him? He held the propeller like a shield.

Behind him, his dark shadow slipped over the sand.

During the war, soldiers had fought here. They'd hidden behind the dunes, firing their rifles. They'd thrown grenades and planted land mines.

The land mines still lay underneath the sand. Sometimes, when the sun shone on them, they exploded from the heat. If someone stepped on a land mine, it tore off his legs. First Uncle had lost his leg that way.

Tinh examined the ground as he walked. What would buried land mines look like? Bumps in the sand? Rough patches? His palms sweated.

He stopped and tilted the soda bottle up to his mouth. He drank all his water.

At last the sand dunes tapered down into the village. The storm had hit here, too. Tinh passed downed trees, damaged houses. As in Hai Nhuan, he saw people working together to clean up.

When a man rode by on a bicycle carrying long sticks of brown-sugar candy, Tinh's mouth watered.

Finally, he spotted the brick hut of the

machine shop, smoke rising from the chimney. Tinh approached and peered inside.

Men wearing thick glasses and masks were gathered around a hot charcoal fire.

One man looked up at Tinh. Walking over, he took the propeller. He touched the sharp, broken edges with his fingertip. "Wait outside," he said, gesturing to a bench. "The storm has brought us a lot of work."

Tinh sat down on the bench, his back against the wall. Even if he had to wait a long time, he'd made it to the machine shop. He'd walked by himself to Phong Chuong and had delivered the propeller.

Tinh felt the heat from the open doorway. Soon, he heard the sound of pounding. He unwrapped his sweet potatoes and peeled them carefully. The pink flesh was soft and sugary.

He ate the peelings, then licked his fingers. By the side of the building, he found a large jar of water and refilled his soda bottle.

Tinh lay down on the bench. He fell asleep to the songs of the birds in the trees overhead.

"Boy," he heard from the air above him. The man was holding the propeller with a pair of tongs. It glowed a dull red. The man laid it on the ground. All three petals were now complete. "Don't touch this yet. It's still hot."

Tinh handed the man the money.

The man gave back a small bill in change.

Tinh watched as the propeller cooled, slowly losing its red tinge. He touched the edge of a blade, then laid his hand on the shaft, now barely warm. He lifted the propeller into his lap and sat with it. This last piece would make the boat whole. This propeller would spin in the water, carrying him and Ba out to the fish.

Now he had to get home.

Just as the town gave way to the sand dunes, Tinh found a small purple flower growing in the shade. He picked it, and gathered bamboo leaves to keep it company. He wrapped the small bouquet with a blade of thin grass.

As he climbed the first sand dune, his heart quickened. Ahead lay a twilight filled with ghosts and unexploded land mines. He began to chant: "*Phat Ba Quan Ahm, see me. . . .*" Balancing the propeller first in one hand, then the other, he wiped his palms on his shirt.

Tinh stopped and stood still. He thought of making the tray of sweet offerings with Banoi at Lunar New Year. He imagined the weight of the tray on his head. He felt Banoi's hand in his as she'd led him to the center of the yard.

While Tinh had held the tray, Banoi sat smiling like the Buddha.

Tinh thought of the Buddha sitting in the temple, now flooded with light. If the real Buddha were here now, he wouldn't be afraid. He'd be walking with his relaxed half smile.

The Buddha knew how to be happy no matter what. Even confronted with danger. Even with the villages and countryside in ruins.

Yet Tinh had turned away from happiness. Why hadn't he stayed and learned the secret of the Buddha's smile?

The sun rode lower.

Tinh took the green pendant from his pocket. As it grew warm in his hand, he imagined the Buddha walking beside him, taking slow, deliberate steps.

Tinh's own steps calmed. His foot landed—heel, then toe—on the copper-colored sand. Then the other foot arrived. The sand closed over the footprints behind him.

By tomorrow the boat would be ready for the ocean once again. But for now, he was just walking over the sand. The repaired propeller and the flower bouquet firmly in his hands, Tinh began to smile.

He was ready to accept the Buddha's diamonds: the first stars, the dome of the sky overhead, the birds hurrying to nest, his own heart beating.

Steadily, Tinh crossed the sand dunes. No ghosts came to torture him. No land mines exploded.

He reached the cemetery as the light faded. He found the gravestones of Banoi and Ong Noi. Kneeling, he laid down his tiny bouquet for his beloved ancestors. Beside it, he laid the pendant. Taking a last look at the Buddha's smile, Tinh walked into the night.

CHAPTER NINE

The next morning, Lan and Ma came to the beach with Tinh and Ba.

Lan wore only a thin bandage now and walked easily, holding Tinh's hand. "Tomorrow we'll build a kite together," he told her.

"A pink one?" she asked.

"That'll depend on what color paper you can find."

"Pink. I have some pink."

Lan and Ma had spent many hours removing the dead fish from the net and mending the holes. Now the nets lay ready in the boat.

As Ba attached the propeller to the engine, he said, “No one could tell that this propeller was once broken.”

Tinh smiled.

Ma and Lan lashed the slim statue to the bow, along with a sprig of leaves and sticks of incense.

The four of them—Third Uncle helping with the final shove—pushed the boat down the sand and into the waves. It floated out, reflected in the water, no longer golden, but a pearly gray.

The storm had changed the boat, Tinh thought. And it had changed him, too.

Ba pulled on the cord, and the engine sprang to life.

As they shoved off—Ma and Lan and Third Uncle waving—Tinh’s heart felt as large as the huge blue ocean. He saw Phu on the shore, the red car in his arms. This bamboo boat, he suddenly realized, was better than one hundred remote-controlled cars.

As they made for the open sea, Tinh lit a stick of incense. The smoke drifted in the light breeze.

When Hai Nhuan was out of sight, Ba silenced the engine.

He and Tinh threw out the nets, then cast the lines.

Tinh waved to Trang Ton in his green boat across the water.

Ba caught a small brown fish and Tinh a huge *ca ngu,* which he pulled in without Ba's help.

"You've caught a bigger fish than I have," Ba said. "You're growing up, Tinh."

Tinh smiled.

When the sun was high overhead, Ba poured diesel into the stove and lit the wood fire.

Tinh put on the pot of water and added the flavorings. Soon, steam rose, hot and fragrant.

"Someday, Tinh, this will be yours." Ba patted the boat.

"Oh, Ba . . ." Tinh leaned forward. "I'll take good care of it. I promise."

When they headed home in the middle of the afternoon, Tinh steered the boat to shore all by himself.

Standing side by side, Ma and Lan waited on the beach, wearing their cone-shaped hats.

When the boat drew close, Tinh ran to the bow and shouted, "There's soup! We have soup!"

Late in the afternoon, Tinh visited the temple.

He tiptoed in.

Although the sky still showed through the gaping roof and the wall of paintings was still damaged, the temple had been cleaned. The photographs of the ancestors were lined neatly on the ancestral altar. The donation box stood upright again.

Someone had laid out dry matches and incense.

Tinh lit a stick of incense and placed it in the bowl of sand in front of the Buddha. As the sweet smoke spiraled, Tinh peeked up.

The spot where people left offerings remained empty. No fruit, no flowers. Yet the Buddha was still at peace, smiling as though he knew a beautiful secret.

Tinh sat down cross-legged on the floor, imitating the position of the Buddha. He placed one hand in the mudra for peace, the other in his lap, close to the earth.

He listened to his breathing. His breath reminded him of waves coming in and out, waves caressing the beach.

He listened to the songs of the birds outside.

The storm-ravaged world settled around Tinh, each part utterly perfect. The sun dropped lower, the rays hitting his back.

Then he heard the sounds of his cousins playing soccer on the field outside.

Tinh stood and bowed three times to the Buddha, pressing his forehead to the earth. After the last bow, he looked into the Buddha's face. The Buddha was right to smile. Tinh smiled back.

Standing in the doorway of the temple, Tinh watched his cousins play. They played like the birds, full of the happiness of the moment.

Tinh walked down the steps between the two stone dragons, calling, "Trang Ton! Dong! Anh! I'm ready to play!"

He ran onto the green field, free of all but the soccer ball and the bright day, the sun balancing on a cloudless blue horizon.

GLOSSARY AND PRONUNCIATION GUIDE

Ba—father

Banoi—grandmother

bodhisattva—one committed to enlightening oneself and others so that all may be liberated from suffering

ca kinh—diamond-shaped fish

ca ngu—large gray fish

ca nuc—small silver fish

cay duong—trees with long needles, pronounced "cay yuong"

chim hai au—seagulls, literally "birds big ocean"

ganh hang—a contraption consisting of a bamboo pole carried over the shoulders with a flat, round basket hanging from each end of the pole

longan—a fruit that grows in clumps. It has a hard, woody skin and a chewy, white center.

Lunar New Year—celebrated either in late January or in February, according to the Chinese lunisolar calendar, which takes into account both lunar and solar cycles of time. Instead of celebrating individual birthdays, all children are one year older on Lunar New Year.

Ma—mother

mudra—hand gesture used in Buddhist meditation

Ong Noi—grandfather

Phat Ba Quan Ahm—the Vietnamese Bodhisattva of Compassion, who began her life as a princess called Wondrous Goodness. Faced with the suffering of the world, she chose to become a nun in order to relieve suffering. Her father, the king, tried to kill her because of her decision. Later on, Wondrous Goodness sacrificed both her arms and both her eyes to heal her father. This Bodhisattva is often depicted as having one thousand arms and one thousand eyes because of her limitless commitment to helping others.

AUTHOR'S NOTE

More than two thousand five hundred years ago, the Buddha was born as a prince named Siddhartha. When he was just a baby, a wise man predicted that he would become enlightened, free from suffering. Siddhartha's father was upset at the prediction as he wanted his son to be a powerful ruler. He kept Siddhartha secluded in the palace so he would know nothing of the world.

Nevertheless, as a child, Siddhartha witnessed worms being eaten by birds. He was shocked and saddened by the worms' pain. He also rescued a swan that his cousin had wounded with an arrow.

The young Siddhartha sat under a rose-apple tree learning to meditate, paying attention to the sensations of his breathing.

In spite of the king's precautions, as a young man Siddhartha went out of the palace. For the first time, he witnessed old age, illness, and death. The sight of suffering moved him so deeply that he escaped from the palace, going into the world to become a holy man.

For years, Siddhartha lived among the holy men of the forests. These men ate almost nothing and tortured themselves, believing that this lifestyle would lead them to the truth. Siddhartha became known as Gautama.

Gautama grew very weak. One day he heard some girls playing a lute, a musical instrument with strings. Upon hearing the music, he realized that if the strings were too tight or too loose the music wouldn't be beautiful. He saw that by living the life of self-denial, he'd pulled his own strings too tight. Gautama resolved to live a life of moderation.

Soon after this realization, Gautama was bathing and almost fainted from hunger. A young girl offered him a bowl of rice and milk.

After Gautama had eaten and gained strength, he recalled his childhood meditations under the rose-apple tree. He seated himself under a bodhi tree, resolving not to move until he had found a way to end suffering.

Gautama sat under the tree for forty-nine days. During this time, he experienced many temptations, but overcame all of them. He gained insight into suffering, understanding that it is caused by greed, selfishness, and ignorance.

Gautama transformed into the Buddha, the Enlightened One. He became a respected teacher. Many people came to hear him speak and to practice the teachings that have now been handed down for more than two thousand five hundred years.

In Buddhism, Buddha is not worshipped as a god. Instead, Buddha statues are used to remind us of the wise and compassionate Buddha nature within ourselves.

The Vietnam War (1959–1975) was a struggle between the communist government of North Vietnam and the American-backed government of South Vietnam.

In order to stop the spread of Communism in southeast Asia, the United States sent troops to Vietnam to fight alongside the South Vietnamese troops.

The war claimed 58,000 American lives and the lives of between 2 million and 5.7 million

Vietnamese, a large number of whom were civilians.

While much of the fighting involved conventional battles and aerial bombing, the Vietnam War was largely a guerilla war affecting the civilian population. In simple villages like Hai Nhuan, soldiers from both sides planted land mines, burned houses, and killed innocent people.

Although in this story the war has been over for several years, Tinh and the other villagers still suffer from the aftermath of the conflict.

ACKNOWLEDGMENTS

I would like to acknowledge the assistance of my friends and fellow writers Gretchen Woelfle, Susan O'Leary, and Emily Whittle; the members of my critique group, Janice Yuwiler, Virginia Loh, and Sarah Wones Tomp; the Venerable Phuoc Tinh of Deer Park Monastery for his inspiring dharma talk on the Buddha's diamonds; and, as always, my editors, Deborah Wayshak and Amy Ehrlich, who helped young Tinh find the Buddha's diamonds. —C. M.

IN POST-WAR ITALY, CAN TWO ORPHAN GIRLS WHO ARE BEST FRIENDS STAY TOGETHER?

Take Me with You
Carolyn Marsden

Susanna and Pina are orphans at the *Instituto di Gesù Bambino*. Growing up together, they can't imagine life without each other. When couples start to visit hoping to find a child to adopt, Susanna is certain Pina, with her blond hair and pale skin, will be chosen at once—unlike Susanna, whose father was a black American soldier and who doesn't look anything like other Italians. The two best friends worry that they'll be separated, but then a surprise visitor arrives. Could this be the miracle that will make both their dreams come true?

★ "Marsden is like a master craftsman, using words instead of stitches for her deceptively simple design."
—*Booklist* (starred review)

Hardcover ISBN 978-0-7636-3739-2

Also by Carolyn Marsden

co-authored with
Virginia Shin-Mui Loh

co-authored with
Philip Matzigeit

www.candlewick.com